Jules Verne (1828-1905)
was born in Nantes, France.

20,000 Leagues under the Sea
was first published in 2 parts in
1869 and 1870.

This edition published in 1994 by
SMITHMARK Publishers Inc.,
16 East 32nd Street, New York,
NY 10016.

SMITHMARK books are available for bulk purchase for
sales promotion and premium use. For details write or call
the manager of special sales, SMITHMARK Publishers Inc.,
16 East 32nd Street, New York,
NY 10016; (212) 532-6600.

Produced by Brompton Books Inc.
15 Sherwood Place
Greenwich, CT 06830

ISBN 0-8317-1566-9

Printed in Hong Kong

10 9 8 7 6 5 4 3 2 1

VAN GOOL'S

20,000 Leagues under the Sea

SMITHMARK

Chapter 1
A DANGEROUS INVITATION

All around the world, from Paris to New York, people were talking about the huge monster that had been terrorising the seas for the past few months. Sailors, scientists and the public argued about it furiously. Was it a living creature, or something made by man? It attacked any ship that came near it, and survivors spoke of its great size, and huge glowing eyes.

My name is Pierre Aronnax and at that time I was a professor at the Natural History Museum in Paris. I had written an article on the monster which had been published in several magazines. I declared that if it was some kind of undersea craft, it must have been built by a government. Yet every government denied owning it. I decided, therefore, that it must simply be an unusually large whale.

Not long after this article was published, I received a letter from the American government inviting me to take part in a research trip on board the *Abraham Lincoln*, a ship built especially for the task. I accepted and my faithful servant, Conseil, accompanied me.

We sailed from New York, and headed for the Pacific Ocean, where the last sighting of the monster had been reported. We spent three months searching but saw no sign of anything unusual. My presence on board amused the crew, who were scornful of the article I'd written. One sailor in particular, Ned Land, took every opportunity to argue with me. A whaler by trade, he was convinced that such a large creature could not exist. "But if I'm proved wrong," he added, "I'll be ready with my harpoon. That's if it ever shows itself!"

One evening, as we were getting ready for bed, we heard Ned cry out, "It's here!" We ran out on deck. In the dark we saw a huge shape, which cast a pale light over the water. We kept a watch all night, but the creature came no closer.

At dawn, the captain of the *Abraham Lincoln* decided to approach the creature. But it always managed to keep its distance. If we got too close, it would disappear under the waves, then re-surface behind us. It seemed to be playing with us.

"Full steam ahead!" cried the captain, but it was no use, we were too slow to keep up.

"Prepare to fire!" he commanded. The cannons boomed, but our cannonballs bounced off the monster's smooth flanks! After a few hours of this game of cat and mouse, the thing seemed to be slowing down.

"Captain, look!" I cried. "We may be able to get closer." Ned lifted his harpoon. As soon as the monster was in range, Ned threw the harpoon as hard as he could. As the weapon touched its side, the monster shuddered. Suddenly torrents of water streamed from its nostrils and swamped our ship. I felt a huge wave lift me up, and I was flung into the sea.

My clothes were weighing me down in the icy water! I struggled frantically, for I was beginning to sink. The *Abraham Lincoln* was disappearing into the distance, and I was sure I was about to die. Suddenly I was seized roughly by the shoulders. "Keep still, Sir. I'm a good swimmer. Just hold on to me."

"Conseil!" I cried, choking on the salty water. "Did you fall overboard too?"

"Not exactly, Sir. I jumped after you. It is my job to follow you wherever you go." I was overcome by Conseil's loyalty to me, but there was no time for words. I felt my strength, and courage, returning.

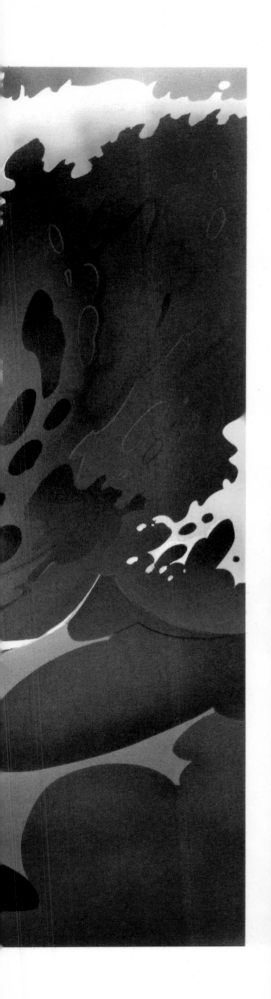

We soon found that there was a third survivor. "Look, Conseil, it's Ned! But what is he holding on to?" In horror we realised – it was the monster! Ned was clinging helplessly to its back. As I looked closer, I saw that it was a very strange animal indeed, for it was made entirely of steel! Ned helped us to climb on. Clinging to the slippery surface, we banged on the sides, hoping that someone would hear us. "Is no one there?" cried Ned. Were we going to be left to drown?

The night passed, and we began to lose hope. But in the morning, a door at the top of the craft opened, and eight uniformed men climbed out. They hauled us to our feet, and thrust us roughly inside.

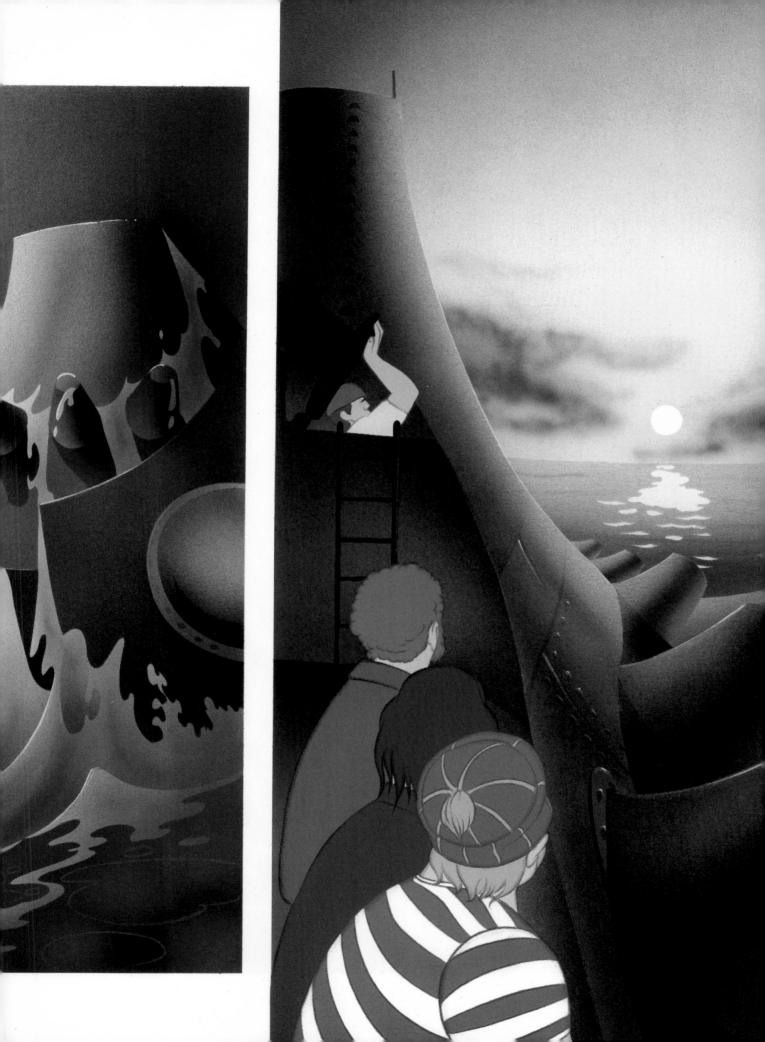

Without a word the men pushed us into a dark room and locked the door. Hours passed before the door opened once more, and a light was switched on. Two men entered. They wore strange clothes, and spoke in a language none of us had ever heard before. We tried to speak to them, but they did not appear to understand English, French or German. Finally, frustrated by their lack of success, the two men left. Shortly afterwards they returned, this time carrying trays of food. We were relieved for by now we were very hungry. The food was delicious, and the portions were generous. "At least these savages aren't planning to starve us to death!" said Ned, eating hungrily. Feeling a little more comfortable, we soon fell asleep.

"Gentlemen, wake up!"

Before us was a tall, distinguished man. He seemed to be in charge, and although he spoke with an accent, his English was perfect.

"Let me introduce myself. I am Captain Nemo. You are on board my submarine, the *Nautilus*. Everything will be done to make you comfortable, but I am afraid you will not be able to leave. Either you accept this situation calmly, or we will be forced to throw you back into the sea." Astounded, Conseil, Ned and myself exchanged glances. Then I replied, "Captain, it seems we have no choice but to obey."

"Excellent. Now, gentlemen, please follow me." He led us into a huge dining room, where the table was laid with fine porcelain and silver. The meal was delicious, but none of the dishes were familiar. "Everything we eat on board the *Nautilus* comes from the sea," explained the captain. "The sea is the richest place in the world. You will soon see for yourselves."

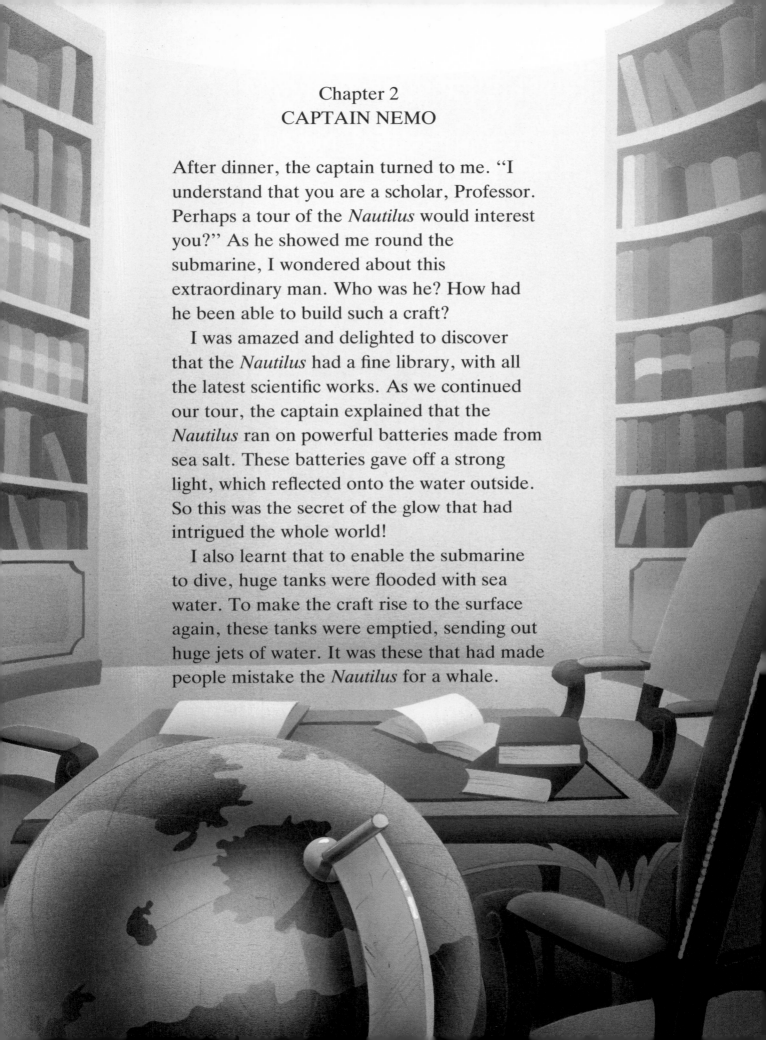

Chapter 2
CAPTAIN NEMO

After dinner, the captain turned to me. "I understand that you are a scholar, Professor. Perhaps a tour of the *Nautilus* would interest you?" As he showed me round the submarine, I wondered about this extraordinary man. Who was he? How had he been able to build such a craft?

I was amazed and delighted to discover that the *Nautilus* had a fine library, with all the latest scientific works. As we continued our tour, the captain explained that the *Nautilus* ran on powerful batteries made from sea salt. These batteries gave off a strong light, which reflected onto the water outside. So this was the secret of the glow that had intrigued the whole world!

I also learnt that to enable the submarine to dive, huge tanks were flooded with sea water. To make the craft rise to the surface again, these tanks were emptied, sending out huge jets of water. It was these that had made people mistake the *Nautilus* for a whale.

"Now, Professor, I must leave you. You will find your friends waiting for you in the salon. Please feel free to explore the *Nautilus* further if you wish." Several hours later, I was trying as best I could to answer Ned's increasingly irritating questions, when suddenly the room was plunged into utter darkness. Silently a panel in the wall slid back, revealing a huge window. Before us was an incredible scene! Shoals of brightly colored fish swam by, while sharks and other strange creatures circled the submarine cautiously. We gazed at the sight in speechless admiration. Then the panel closed once more, and the lights came back on.

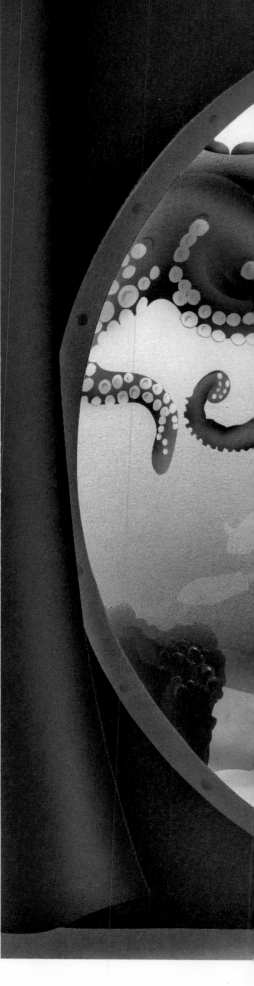

Our days began to settle into a routine. Most of my time was spent studying in the library, or exploring the ship. We did not see much of Captain Nemo, but one evening I found a note from him in my cabin: "Would you all like to come hunting tomorrow morning on the island of Crespo?"

Excited at the thought of walking on solid ground once more, we were ready and waiting when the captain came to collect us. To our surprise, he explained that the island of Crespo had been submerged thousands of years ago! We were to walk on the bottom of the sea! But how would we breathe?

Sturdy diving suits, equiped with bottles of oxygen, were waiting for us in the airlock. Ned was horrified, and refused to join us.

"Put on that infernal machine?" he asked fearfully, "Never!"

Conseil and I followed the captain away from the submarine and I looked around me in wonder. I recognised many plants and creatures, but I had only before seen them in the pages of a book. But there was no time to waste – there was work to be done. Each armed with a compressed air gun, we caught plenty of fish.

The captain spoke the truth when he said that the sea is the richest place in the world. But it is also one of the most dangerous! We were attacked by a group of hungry sharks, and only just managed to escape the sharp claws of a huge crab.

Since boarding the *Nautilus*, my life had been so exciting that I was almost glad to have been taken prisoner!

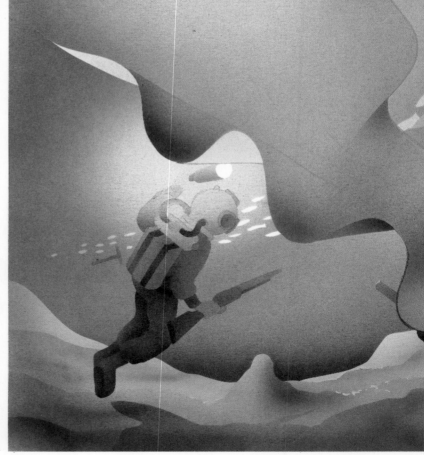

Chapter 3
NED IS ANGRY

Only poor Ned did not appreciate life on board.

"Listen to me, Professor," he cried one day, "I can't take any more of this fish and all this water! I want a nice steak, and a large whisky! And what about bread? How long is it since we last ate bread? We must escape!"

Our discussion was interrupted by a great shudder which passed through the *Nautilus*. I ran to ask the captain what had happened, and pointing to his charts he explained that we had come aground on a coral reef by an island. "It's nothing to worry about," he said. "The tides should free us in three or four days." This immediately gave Ned an idea. "Can we go ashore?" he begged. "I'd give anything to stand on solid ground, and have a chance to hunt some proper food!"

The captain agreed. "But listen," he said, "you must go alone. My men and I have vowed never to set foot on land again."

Conseil and I went with Ned in the canoe. We had three days to explore the island, and Ned was delighted – there was plenty of fruit and game. Every evening we camped out in the open. On the third day, we were just finishing our evening meal when Ned declared, "We're much better off on this lost island than on board that wretched *Nautilus*." The words had hardly left his mouth when an arrow whizzed by his ear! It was followed by a barrage of stones and arrows which drove us to our canoe. Natives!

"Captain!" I cried as we approached the submarine. "We're being attacked!"

Captain Nemo stood in the doorway. "Quickly, get inside," he said. "The tide will carry us away in a few minutes."

I was shocked by his calmness. "But Captain . . . the natives!" "What about them?" he asked.

"They are climbing on board!"

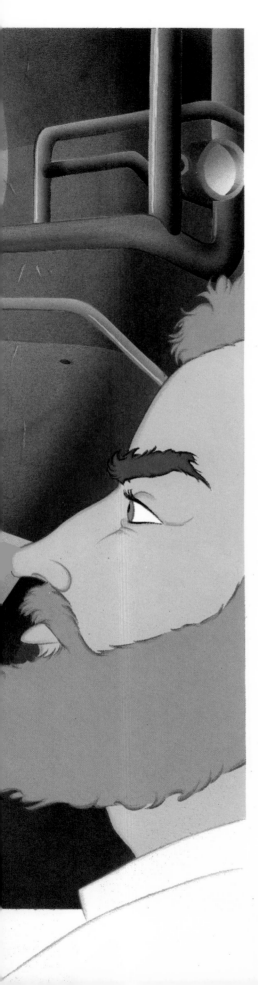

"They won't get far," replied Nemo. As soon as we were inside, he pressed a button. One of the natives, braver than the rest, stepped onto the ladder. Suddenly he let out a great cry of pain and fell backwards. Howling in terror, the natives ran from the *Nautilus*, while we watched in astonishment. Suddenly I understood. "These steps are made of metal!" I cried. "And you passed an electric current through them!"

The captain shrugged, then turned his back and gave the command to leave.

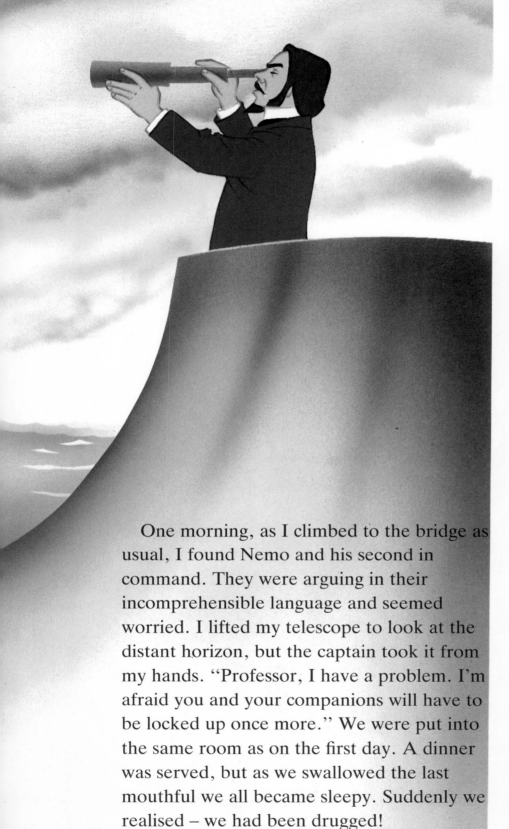

One morning, as I climbed to the bridge as usual, I found Nemo and his second in command. They were arguing in their incomprehensible language and seemed worried. I lifted my telescope to look at the distant horizon, but the captain took it from my hands. "Professor, I have a problem. I'm afraid you and your companions will have to be locked up once more." We were put into the same room as on the first day. A dinner was served, but as we swallowed the last mouthful we all became sleepy. Suddenly we realised – we had been drugged!

Much later, I was woken by cries: "Professor! Professor!" The captain was shaking my shoulder desperately. "Get up! You are a doctor, aren't you? Follow me, I beg you."

The captain led me to a cabin. On the bed lay a young man, moaning in pain. There was a terrible wound in his head. I examined him, but it was hopeless. "Captain, this man is seriously injured. He will not survive." The captain was silent, but I saw a tear slide down his cheek. This seemingly cold man had a heart after all! As I had expected, the man died during the day. We never learnt how the young sailor had been injured.

The next day another surprise awaited us. Putting on our diving suits, we followed the captain and the crew for several hours. Finally we came to a coral reef, and to my astonishment, it was covered with crosses. This was the underwater cemetery of the *Nautilus* crew!

One morning, a few weeks later, the captain knocked at my cabin door. "Professor," he said, "we are near the island of Ceylon, and there is something I would like to show you." As we set out on this new underwater expedition, I was burning with curiosity. We came to a cave in the rocks, and I gasped in surprise – inside was an enormous oyster, its shell partly open. Captain Nemo gently slid the blade of his knife into the gap and beckoned me forward. Peering inside I saw a huge pearl – it must have been the size of a coconut! I reached out my hand to touch it, but the captain stopped me. Pulling out his knife, he let the shell close again. I realised that he had decided to leave the enormous pearl to grow.

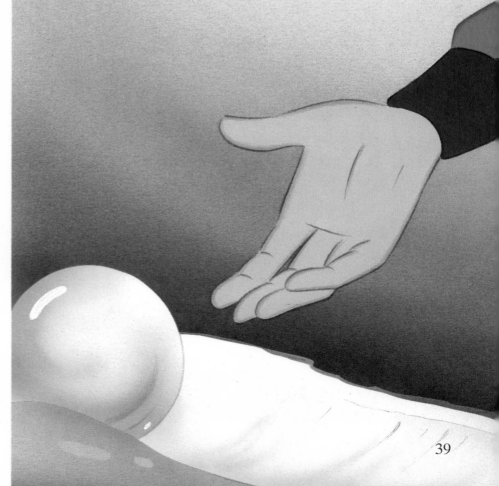

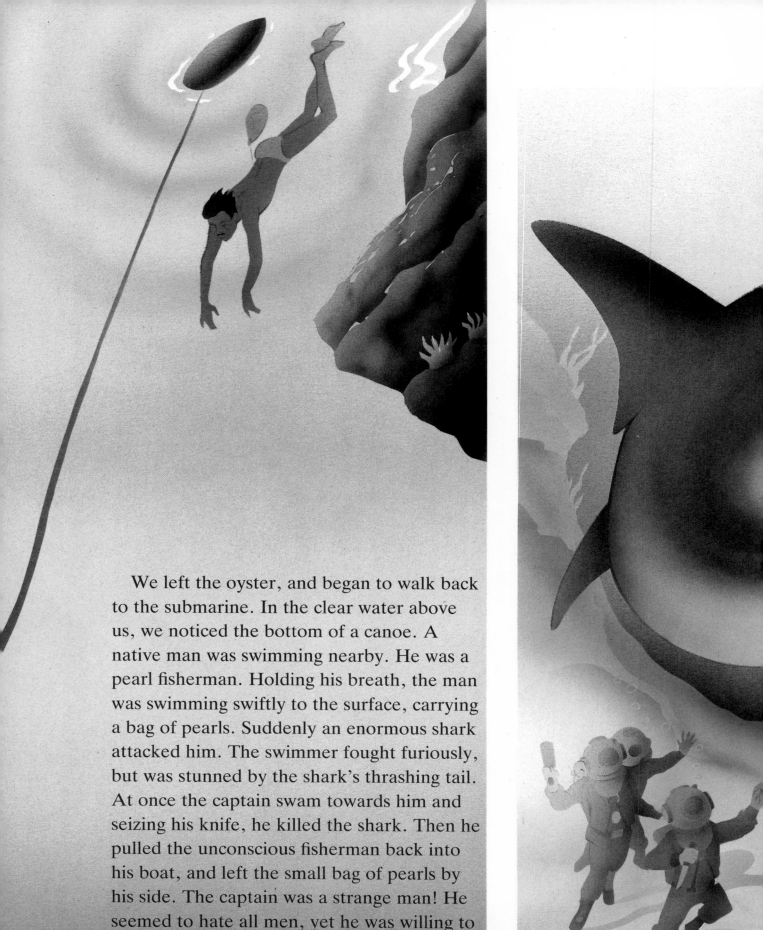

We left the oyster, and began to walk back to the submarine. In the clear water above us, we noticed the bottom of a canoe. A native man was swimming nearby. He was a pearl fisherman. Holding his breath, the man was swimming swiftly to the surface, carrying a bag of pearls. Suddenly an enormous shark attacked him. The swimmer fought furiously, but was stunned by the shark's thrashing tail. At once the captain swam towards him and seizing his knife, he killed the shark. Then he pulled the unconscious fisherman back into his boat, and left the small bag of pearls by his side. The captain was a strange man! He seemed to hate all men, yet he was willing to come to their rescue when they were helpless!

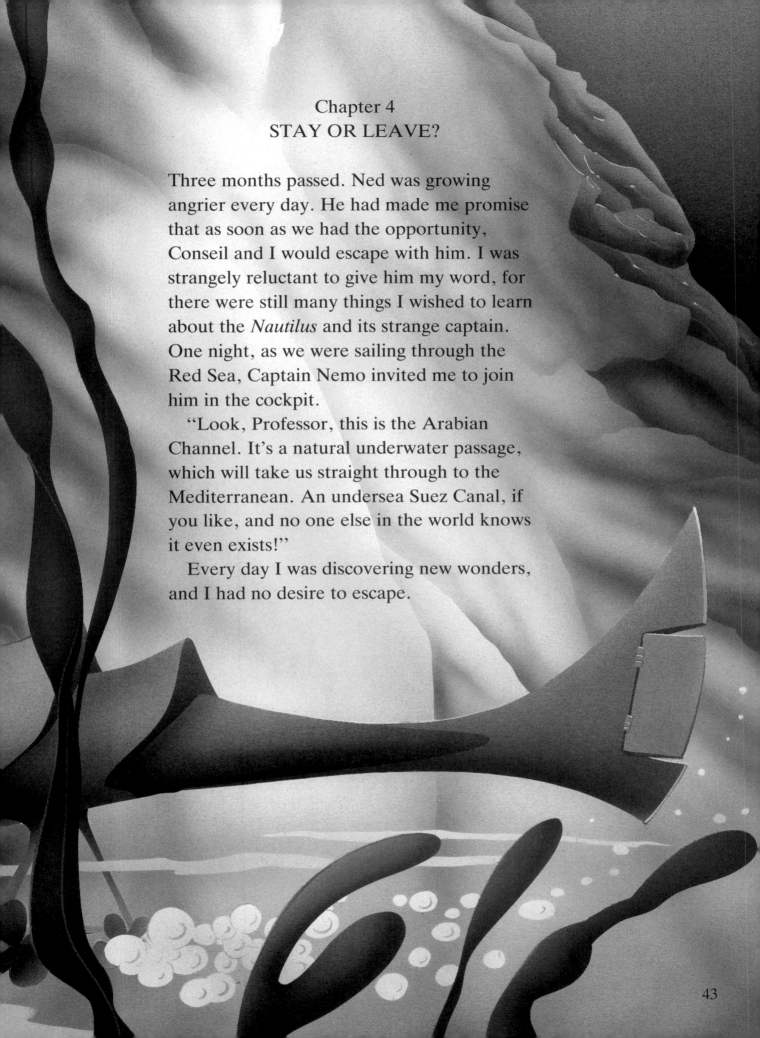

Chapter 4
STAY OR LEAVE?

Three months passed. Ned was growing angrier every day. He had made me promise that as soon as we had the opportunity, Conseil and I would escape with him. I was strangely reluctant to give him my word, for there were still many things I wished to learn about the *Nautilus* and its strange captain. One night, as we were sailing through the Red Sea, Captain Nemo invited me to join him in the cockpit.

"Look, Professor, this is the Arabian Channel. It's a natural underwater passage, which will take us straight through to the Mediterranean. An undersea Suez Canal, if you like, and no one else in the world knows it even exists!"

Every day I was discovering new wonders, and I had no desire to escape.

Several days later we were looking out of the great window when a man came into view, swimming in the clear waters of the Mediterranean. He approached the window, and signalled to Captain Nemo. Nemo nodded, and went over to a large chest. He opened it briefly, and we saw to our surprise that it was full of gold pieces! Nemo shut and locked the chest, then called to his men. Two crew members came in and carried the chest away. A little later I heard the sound of the canoe setting out to sea. I began to question the captain, but he stopped me. "I will wish you goodnight, Professor," he said, then turned and disappeared into his cabin.

Who was the man who had come to collect the gold pieces? And where did the captain get them from?

Two days later, we had passed through the straits of Gibraltar, and we were travelling some distance out from Portugal. Captain Nemo came to find me.

"Professor," he began, unrolling some ancient charts. "We are now in the bay of Vigo. In 1702 a fleet of Spanish galleons was sunk here by the English. Now do you understand where my treasure comes from?" Without waiting for my reply, the captain activated the panel in the salon. What I saw outside astounded me. The crewmen from the *Nautilus* were exploring the sunken ships, and carrying back sacks full of gold and silver. "There's enormous wealth here," continued Nemo, "and I put it to good use. My men and I distribute it among the poor people of the world!" He stopped abruptly, as if he had said too much. But his eyes shone, and his voice trembled with emotion.

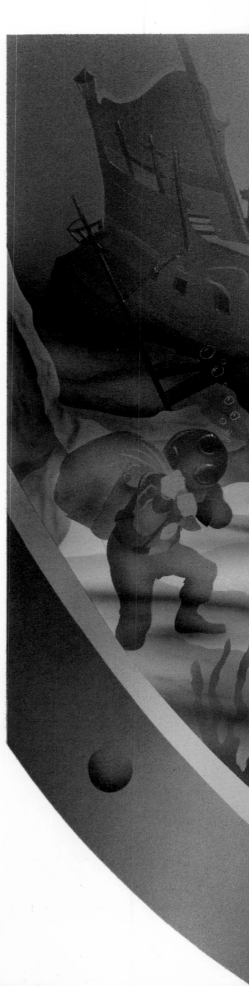

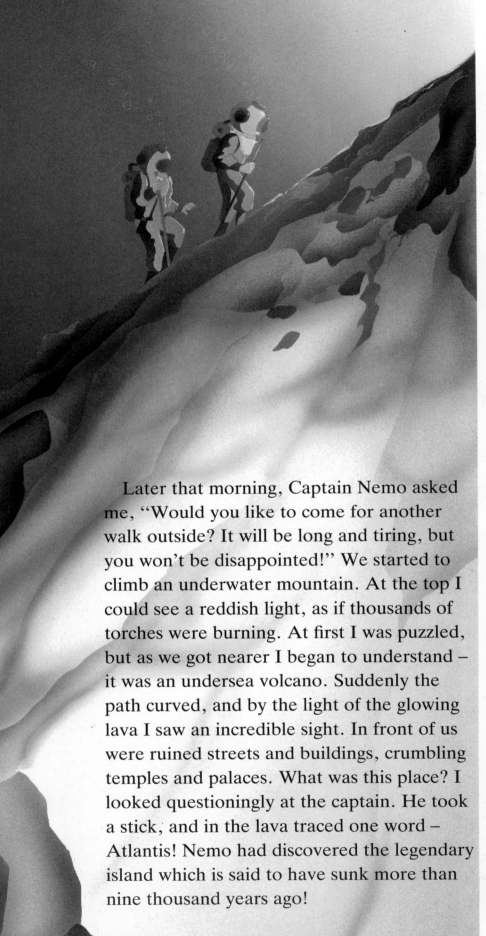

Later that morning, Captain Nemo asked
me, "Would you like to come for another
walk outside? It will be long and tiring, but
you won't be disappointed!" We started to
climb an underwater mountain. At the top I
could see a reddish light, as if thousands of
torches were burning. At first I was puzzled,
but as we got nearer I began to understand –
it was an undersea volcano. Suddenly the
path curved, and by the light of the glowing
lava I saw an incredible sight. In front of us
were ruined streets and buildings, crumbling
temples and palaces. What was this place? I
looked questioningly at the captain. He took
a stick, and in the lava traced one word –
Atlantis! Nemo had discovered the legendary
island which is said to have sunk more than
nine thousand years ago!

Our next destination was the South Pole. Captain Nemo had decided that he would be the first man to set foot at this desolate spot. Other expeditions had made the attempt, but all had failed.

After several days one of the crew came to him. "Captain, we can't go any further. The ice is blocking our path."

"Then we must dive," ordered the captain. "If we cannot get through the ice, we will go under it."

Finally we reached the Pole, and followed Captain Nemo out onto the ice. Almost hidden by the swirling snow, he planted his flag firmly at the exact centre of the Pole. What a triumph!

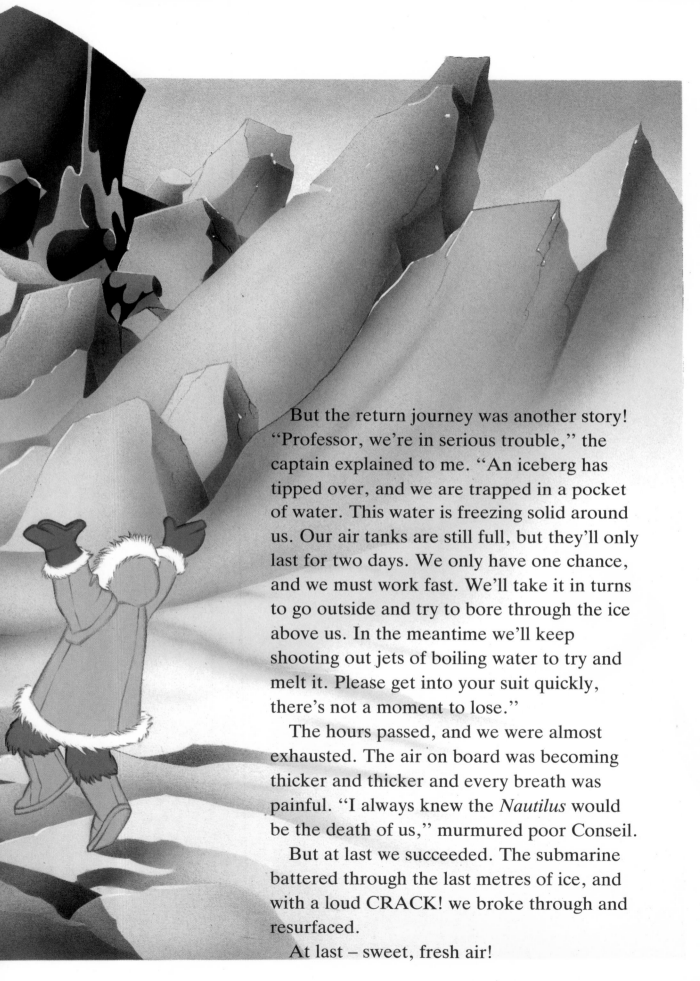

But the return journey was another story!
"Professor, we're in serious trouble," the
captain explained to me. "An iceberg has
tipped over, and we are trapped in a pocket
of water. This water is freezing solid around
us. Our air tanks are still full, but they'll only
last for two days. We only have one chance,
and we must work fast. We'll take it in turns
to go outside and try to bore through the ice
above us. In the meantime we'll keep
shooting out jets of boiling water to try and
melt it. Please get into your suit quickly,
there's not a moment to lose."

The hours passed, and we were almost
exhausted. The air on board was becoming
thicker and thicker and every breath was
painful. "I always knew the *Nautilus* would
be the death of us," murmured poor Conseil.

But at last we succeeded. The submarine
battered through the last metres of ice, and
with a loud CRACK! we broke through and
resurfaced.

At last – sweet, fresh air!

Chapter 5
THE ESCAPE

One day we were sailing through the North Sea when the lookouts spotted a huge octopus that was following us. The captain was alarmed. "Get us out of here!" he cried. "We're in great danger." But it was already too late! The monster attacked, and clung to the *Nautilus* with its huge tentacles, blocking the propellers. We were held fast. "If we don't get away quickly, we will be dragged to the bottom of the sea!" cried Nemo. "We must free those propellers!" The crew rushed onto the bridge, armed with knives and harpoons. Suddenly a giant tentacle reached up and curled around one of the sailors. He shouted and struggled, but the octopus dragged him under the water. With a cry of rage, the sailors threw themselves on the monster, fighting furiously until we were free.

After our battle with the octopus, Captain Nemo became more and more distant. The death of the sailor had distressed him deeply. One night I noticed him in his cabin, sitting before a picture of a young woman and two little children. He was weeping softly. What was the captain's secret? What had happened to make him hate the world above the sea?

That same evening, we spotted a ship in the distance. "It's a warship," declared Ned, "But I can't tell what country it comes from." Without warning the warship opened fire on us. "Quickly, Captain, we must dive at once!" I cried. Captain Nemo looked at me scornfully, a strange expression on his face. To our horror he set *Nautilus* on a collision course. We rammed the warship at full speed, ripping a hole in the bottom. Without turning back, we sailed away, leaving the helpless ship sinking behind us.

Some days later, still shocked by what we'd seen, Conseil, Ned and I were discussing the captain. "He is a cruel man," said Conseil. "Those sailors didn't stand a chance." I agreed, then added, "I've not seen any of the crew since that terrible day. They seem to be avoiding us."

"This is our chance to escape," cried Ned.

"You're right, Ned." I replied with a sigh. "I don't think I'll ever understand Captain Nemo's secret now." That night we crept into the canoe and untied it. As we released the last rope, we heard shouts from inside.

"A storm! A storm!" Caught in a raging whirlwind, the canoe was carried away from the *Nautilus*, which disappeared under the waves. In our struggle to remain afloat, one of the oars struck me, and I was knocked unconscious.

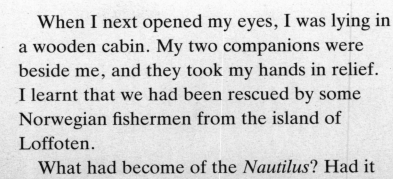

When I next opened my eyes, I was lying in a wooden cabin. My two companions were beside me, and they took my hands in relief. I learnt that we had been rescued by some Norwegian fishermen from the island of Loffoten.

What had become of the *Nautilus*? Had it escaped the storm? Who was Captain Nemo? Where did he come from? Who were the sailors who had chosen to live under the sea with him? To this very day, these questions have remained unanswered. . . .